MAXIMILIAN P. MOUSE, TIME TRAVELER

THE MIGHTY MAXIMILIAN

SAMUEL CLEMENS'S TRAVELING COMPANION

BOOK 4

Philip M. Horender • Guy Wolek

visit us at www.abdopublishing.com

For my friends & colleagues for their hard work and sacrifice in the noblest of professions—PMH

Published by Magic Wagon, a division of the ABDO Group, PO Box 398166, Minneapolis, Minnesota 55439. Copyright © 2014 by Abdo Consulting Group, Inc. International copyrights reserved in all countries. All rights reserved. No part of this book may be reproduced in any form without written permission from the publisher.

Calico Chapter Books™ is a trademark and logo of Magic Wagon.

Printed in the United States of America, North Mankato, Minnesota.
052013
092013

 This book contains at least 10% recycled materials.

Text by Philip M. Horender
Illustrations by Guy Wolek
Edited by Stephanie Hedlund and Rochelle Baltzer
Cover and interior design by Neil Klinepier

Library of Congress Cataloging-in-Publication Data

Horender, Philip M.
  The mighty Maximilian : Samuel Clemens's traveling companion / by Philip M. Horender ; illustrated by Guy Wolek.
     p. cm. -- (Maximilian P. Mouse, time traveler ; bk. 4)
  Summary: Low on fuel, Maximilian's time machine lands him on a Mississippi riverboat where he meets a friendly southern bullfrog, collects an autograph from the author Samuel Clemens to add to his souvenirs, and gets enough fuel to continue his journey through history.
  ISBN 978-1-61641-960-8
1. Twain, Mark, 1835-1910--Juvenile fiction. 2. Mice--Juvenile fiction. 3. Bullfrog--Juvenile fiction. 4. Time travel--Juvenile fiction. 5. Riverboats--Juvenile fiction. 6. Mississippi River--History--19th century--Juvenile fiction. [1. Twain, Mark, 1835-1910--Fiction. 2. Mice--Fiction. 3. Bullfrog--Fiction. 4. Frogs--Fiction. 5. Time travel--Fiction. 6. Adventure and adventurers--Fiction. 7. Riverboats--Fiction. 8. Mississippi River--History--19th century--Fiction.] I. Wolek, Guy, ill. II. Title.
  PZ7.H78087Mig 2013
  813.6--dc23   2012050864

TABLE OF CONTENTS

Chapter 1:
WARNING!

When the time machine began to slow down, Maximilian opened his eyes. Once again, he undid his restraints and carefully opened the portal with his handkerchief. Suddenly, a strange light came on next to the fuel gauge and a buzzer sounded overhead.

Maximilian's stomach dropped. He fought to make out what the lettering said. He was able to see the words *low fuel*.

His head was wildly dizzy from the spinning. Through the moisture on the hatch, he could just barely read words outside on a partially rusted sign. It read: *Mississippi Belle*.

Maximilian struggled to compose himself and drew in a deep breath. *Think . . . think . . .*

The warning signal continued to blink in the darkness of the time machine. Outside, Maximilian could hear talking. The accents were strange to him. He was also beginning to make out music. It was faint, but it was definitely music and people making merry.

Maximilian closed the hatch and tried hard to concentrate. Space was limited inside the time portal. Maximilian dug through his few belongings in search of his beloved journal. He did not remember making any specific notes regarding fuel or time machine maintenance, but he was desperate. At this point, he realized, his options were limited.

Maximilian's tiny paws shook as he flipped through the diary's pages. Occasionally he licked his finger in order to separate the pages more easily. He glanced past his notes on President Abraham Lincoln, past his discovery of gold in Silver Springs, and past his entry on the driving of the golden spike at Promontory Point.

Maximilian's luck had taken a **drastic** change for the worse in a short time. He had yet to get used to the roller coaster of emotions he experienced from one leg of his trip to the next. Now he found himself in the most serious situation of his young life.

Maximilian carefully placed his journal back in his backpack and closed his eyes. He could picture Nathaniel pacing in his workshop, telling Maximilian all about the time machine.

Why couldn't he remember what Nathaniel had said about fuel?

The exterior of the capsule was an acorn shell. It had been polished to help keep it aligned during time travel, but that's all he could remember. Maximilian's muscles relaxed and he slowly fell asleep.

While Maximilian slept, the large steam-engine paddleboat that he had come to rest on was slowly coming to life. The **hydraulics** began spewing steam. They worked hard to turn the large wooden-planked paddle from its resting position. Slowly, the *Mississippi Belle* pulled away from the port.

Chapter 2:
ABOARD THE BELLE

Maximilian dreamed for the first time since he had begun his trip. The cool summer breeze danced its way through the grass. The glen was filled with seasonal flowers and alive with bees and butterflies.

Maximilian loved this time in Tanner's Glen the most. He **cherished** the days he was allowed to play the day away and not worry about chores. He sat peacefully on the bank of Farmer Tanner's winding, lazy creek.

From his seat on the creek bank, Maximilian peered into a break in the line of trees in the fence row. The trees cast a dark shadow over the entire glen. Maximilian could sense something was there in the darkness. He strained his eyes and tried to make out what awaited him in the forest, just out of his sight. He looked deeper and began to see a form take shape. He could almost make out what the shape was.

Maximilian reluctantly opened his eyes. It didn't take him long to realize he was not at home in the glen, but in the time machine. He still had an empty fuel cell and no way to travel home.

For a moment, Maximilian thought about closing his eyes once again. He could try to make his way back into the dream he had just left. Instead, he decided to think more about his fuel problem.

The capsule's window was tinted glass. So, it was difficult for Maximilian to see whether it was day or night out. He carefully opened the hatch and leaned out.

Maximilian's long, wiry whiskers fluttered in an attempt to gather information about his new surroundings. He pulled himself from the pod and patted the dust from his shirt.

The time machine had come to rest next to a large flotation device made from some strange material. The ring was tied to a heavy rope.

The round **buoy** was painted with the boat's name—*Mississippi Belle*.

Maximilian began putting together the pieces to the puzzle. He was on the deck of a moving boat. He turned his face into the soft breeze. The warm air felt refreshing after being in the time machine for so long.

Maximilian slowly made his way out from underneath a bench. An impressive sight was not ten yards in front of him. A massive paddle wheel churned its way slowly through the water. It threw a cool, crisp mist into the air as it turned.

Maximilian's eyes grew bigger. He slowly backed himself underneath the bench again. Something about the size and scale of the wheel scared Maximilian. It was like a slow-moving giant wading through the water.

Large wooden planks worked to power the *Mississippi Belle* through the currents. The planks were whitewashed and fastened securely into place by large, iron bolts. Air released from the hydraulic **compressors** sounded like the breathing of a hibernating bear.

Maximilian had become used to something very similar to this paddle wheel back home in Tanner's Glen. Over the years, Farmer Tanner had expanded his farm. He had added an old pine waterwheel that helped grind grain to make flour. Maximilian had spent days watching the waterwheel turn. He had studied it very closely. He began to see many similarities between Farmer Tanner's mill wheel and that of the riverboat.

After a few minutes of watching the paddle wheel, Maximilian took in the rest of his surroundings. The boat passed large, low-hanging trees draped in moss.

Even with the noise created by the paddle wheel, Maximilian could hear music and talking. Although the music was soft, Maximilian recognized some of the songs. He could not quite put his paw on exactly what songs they were though.

What kind of boat is this? Maximilian wondered as he pondered his next move.

A scrap of paper suddenly fell into Maximilian's paws. He took a moment to read it as his pocket watch reminded him what time it was. It was still the morning—ten o'clock to be exact.

Maximilian read the simple, typed script:

Ticket exchangeable for one seat aboard the Mississippi Belle: *Vicksburg, Mississippi, to the Port of New Orleans, Louisiana.*

"New Orleans," Maximilian mumbled. He read the boat ticket a second time. Its one end had been torn when its passenger had boarded earlier that morning. Maximilian breathed a heavy sigh of disappointment and placed a paw on his hip.

The possessor of this ticket should board at 7:30 a.m. at the Port of Vicksburg on Saturday, December 24, 1875.

Chapter 3:
BOGIE

It was Christmas Eve. Somehow that made not making it home that much more painful. The small field mouse sat motionless on the deck of the Mississippi paddleboat in shock.

Maximilian watched as a large fly landed on the wooden railing of the boat. Coarse, dark hair covered its body and its bulging eyes darted from one end of the deck to the other. Finally, those eyes fell squarely on Maximilian. It looked him over as its wings shook to dry themselves.

What is it looking at? Maximilian thought uneasily.

The fly began to make its way down the railing toward Maximilian. Maximilian felt more and more uneasy.

Should he move? What could an oversized, sluggish black fly possibly want with him?

Maximilian grew more and more nervous as the fly made its way closer and closer to him.

And then, before Maximilian even knew what was happening, the fly was gone! Maximilian blinked hard and rubbed his eyes with his paws. What had happened to the fly?

Maximilian peered around the corner of the boat. He was immediately confronted with the enormous grin of a bullfrog. He had never seen a frog so big before in his life. Both he and the frog jumped with surprise. Maximilian nearly fell over entirely.

"Well, I'll be a Cajun grasshopper on a hot July skillet!" the startled bullfrog declared. His huge, dark green body glistened with sweat. Maximilian nearly laughed out loud when he realized the frog was wearing denim overalls.

"I apologize," Maximilian managed to say, his heart still racing. "I . . . I had no idea you were there," he said.

The frog removed his wide-brimmed straw hat. "No need to apologize, my fair mouse," he said with a smile. "That was one of the best jumps this ol' frog has had in a long while."

Maximilian was relieved at the frog's reaction. He certainly was a sight to see. Maximilian immediately liked him.

"I'll be!" the frog continued, patting his chest now with the straw hat. "Now, where is my Southern **hospitality**?" the frog said. He extended a webbed hand in Maximilian's direction.

"The name is Bogart T. Bullfrog," the happy amphibian said proudly, "but you can call me Bogie."

"It's very nice to make your **acquaintance**," Maximilian said. He gave the frog the firmest handshake he could muster.

"Just out of curiosity, how long exactly have you been standing around that corner?" Bogie asked, his eyes falling toward the ground. A hint of embarrassment could be detected in his voice. Maximilian was beginning to realize where Bogie's line of questioning was headed.

"Oh, not long," Maximilian fibbed. "Not long at all."

Bogie shook his head as his green cheeks began to turn a light shade of red. "I only ask," Bogie explained, "because I just finished having a late breakfast. Some have described it as somewhat **unsavory**."

The image of the large, hairy fly was still fresh in Maximilian's mind. He swallowed hard. His stomach turned at the mere idea of Bogie having eaten it for breakfast.

"Well, this is my first time on a riverboat. I was far too distracted by the paddle wheel to have noticed anything else," Maximilian said. His lie fooled the frog. Bogie's eyes slowly rose to meet Maximilian's again.

"First time on a riverboat?" Bogie said in amazement. "Then, consider me your personal tour guide aboard the majestic *Mississippi Belle*!"

Maximilian hesitated to leave the time machine unattended yet again. But, he decided that a tour of the boat might actually jog his memory. He had to figure out what fuel he needed for the time machine.

"I would certainly love to see more of the ship," Maximilian said.

"Shucks, I wouldn't consider myself much of a Southern gentle-frog if I didn't give my new friend a tour of the vessel I call home for almost three months out of the year," Bogie said. He adjusted one of his overall straps. "You'll be amazed at the stories I have to tell you about the *Belle*."

Maximilian snuck one last glance at the time machine. Then, he and Bogie began their way down the boardwalk of the *Mississippi Belle*'s lower tier.

The size of the riverboat surprised Maximilian. He really had no idea of how large it was from the rear of the boat. It was impressive to think of how powerful the paddle wheel must be in order to move a vessel this size.

"Are you from N'Orleans?" Bogie pried in a hard Southern drawl.

"No, I'm not from around here," Maximilian replied. "But I'm hoping I can get home from here."

Bogie stopped and gave Maximilian a confused look at the riddle he had just heard. But he said nothing.

"Well, you definitely chose a historic time to join us," Bogie said. "This leg from Vicksburg to N'Orleans will be the final dance for the *Belle* along her beloved Mississippi River."

"Really?" Maximilian said, somewhat surprised. "The boat looks like it's almost brand-new."

The railings they passed by were draped with garland. The windows they walked under were dressed with wreaths and other decorations celebrating the Christmas season.

When the pair came to a small opening, they stopped.

"You're right, Maximilian, the boat itself is in perfect condition," Bogie said. "See, the **transcontinental** railroad was completed a few years back. It has made the train very popular, which has really taken its toll on the number of people traveling by paddleboat."

Bogie hopped through the opening and motioned for Maximilian to follow him. "Come, Maximilian," Bogie said from underneath his straw cap. "This is where our tour will begin."

Chapter 4:
A STERNWHEELER

"**R**ivers such as the muddy Mississippi have been an important way of transporting goods and people for quite some time. With the invention of steam power, rivers became the central way around our beloved US of A," the bullfrog said. He was making his way with surprising ease throughout a maze of stairways.

"Of course, the boat we're on right now is far superior to many of the earlier steamships," Bogie continued. "Boats have gotten bigger and better. Oil and coal replaced wood for fuel. And just like that, a trip on a fancy paddler has become an adventure in itself!"

Bogie and Maximilian walked out onto a second open balcony. They were now on a floor similar to the earlier one. However, this floor was enclosed.

"We're on the boiler deck now," Bogie informed Maximilian. "The one before was the main deck. This deck holds the boiler that delivers steam to the entire ship."

Bogie hopped ahead of Maximilian and pointed toward the rear of the deck. "The kitchen is also located on this deck," Bogie said. "Because the threat of fires is so real, the **architects** tried to keep everything that required the boiler power close."

Maximilian shook his head, trying to take in all the information Bogie was feeding him. He immediately noticed that there were more people on this deck. This concerned him.

"Is this the top deck?" Maximilian asked as he glanced up at the finely polished slotted wood panels.

Bogie's attention had been sidetracked for a moment by a purple dragonfly. Bogie was aware again of Maximilian's stare. "No, no," he said. "We still have one more floor above us. It is the **hurricane roof**," he said. His eyes looked up and down the walkway.

"Where are we going exactly?" Maximilian asked. Bogie paused, then caught sight of what he had been looking for.

"Right over here," Bogie said. He hopped toward the front of the boat. "This is one of the best sights anywhere on the ship. One that you will certainly appreciate."

It was still morning and the passengers on the boat were beginning to leave their **statehouses**. Some of the women Maximilian saw were dressed in stunning gowns with **parasols** on their shoulders. The men wore handsome suits and strolled slowly with walking canes. Other passengers had on simpler clothes, giving Maximilian the impression that they were not as wealthy.

Maximilian found himself at the front of the boiler deck. He was looking outward at two massive support beams. Both of the beams extended outward toward the water at about twenty degree angles. They were held in place with many cables and wires.

"I cannot get over how impressive this boat is," Maximilian said. The **compliment** pleased

Bogie, whose smile grew even larger. Beads of sweat dotted Bogie's forehead. Maximilian noticed that one of the denim straps over his shoulder had managed to unhook itself.

Maximilian meant his praise of the *Mississippi Belle*. From their perch on the boiler deck, they could see below them onto the main deck. It was now bustling with activity. The steamship was grand enough on its own, and the beautiful holiday decorations made it truly breathtaking.

"Wait until you see the smokestacks," Bogie said, looking at Maximilian. *"Hew wee!"* Bogie cried. "Why, they reach so far in the sky you almost think you could use them to climb right onto the clouds themselves!"

The boat continued to move at a fairly slow pace. It moved with the currents of the river and tried to avoid any unexpected **debris** that might be in the water.

"This here ship is what we call a 'sternwheeler,'" Bogie continued, again taking the lead as tour guide and paddleboat expert. "It depends entirely on one steam-powered paddle wheel located at the stern—that means the back—of the ship," he explained.

Bogie used just the right mixture of **layman**'s terms and seafaring words for Maximilian to understand.

"Other ships on the Mississippi have a pair of wheels located on either side of the ferry," Bogie said. "They're referred to as 'sidewheelers' and are better for boating down wide rivers like the Missouri," he said. "They're broader and don't change course as well as a sternwheeler does."

Maximilian continued to listen to Bogie's every word, but he was distracted. He noticed a man standing at the railing just below them. The man stood watching the world pass by from the main deck. He wore a brilliant white suit and a neatly pressed, black necktie. The suit coordinated perfectly with his flowing pearl-colored hair and mustache.

Maximilian thought about what might bring a man like that on the *Mississippi Belle.* He could not help but imagine what great adventure he might be on.

Bogie nudged Maximilian and motioned toward another set of stairs. The steps led upward through the ceiling and onto the hurricane roof.

Maximilian nodded at Bogie. When he looked back, the white-suited mystery man was gone.

Chapter 5:
A TOUR
OF THE SHIP

Maximilian and Bogie made their way up the next flight of stairs to the hurricane roof. They hugged the side of the steps in order to avoid being stepped on.

The breeze was much stronger out on the top deck. The two large, black smokestacks **dominated** the hurricane deck. They certainly did not disappoint Maximilian. They looked like towering twins, sending clouds of black smoke trailing behind the ship. The smokestacks reminded Maximilian of the old oak trees in Tanner's Glen.

Bogie must have been able to tell how amazed Maximilian was by the expression on his face. "They really are something!" Bogie said in Maximilian's direction. "I always leave them for last when I show someone the ship. The best for last, you could say!"

Maximilian could now see that all of the cables rigged to the front of the ship were connected to the smokestacks. They formed a network that resembled a spiderweb. Several birds sat perched on these cables. They seemed to be enjoying the lazy river cruise as much as those who had purchased tickets.

"There," Bogie said, once again pointing out something to Maximilian. "That is called the pilot house. It is where the captain steers the ship."

The pilot house that Bogie referred to was small compared to the rest of the boat. It sat behind the smokestacks. It rested on top of the rooms located on the hurricane roof.

"How long would you say the *Mississippi Belle* is?" asked Maximilian, squinting into the sun.

Bogie placed a finger on his chin and thought for a moment. "I would estimate that it would almost have to be 100 yards in length, from stern to bow. Give or take a few feet," he said shaking his head.

"How many people does it carry?" Maximilian asked.

"As far as passengers go," Bogie said, "I think she carries close to 100 people. There are nearly thirty-five crew numbers."

Bogie removed a bright red handkerchief from his denim breast pocket and wiped the sweat from his brow. "It wasn't too long ago that most of the workers on a boat like this would be slaves," Bogie said. "These boats helped create cities like St. Louis and Shreveport, you know."

Maximilian pictured President Lincoln writing his Gettysburg Address into the wee hours of the night.

"Why, the Civil War is still very fresh in the minds of those who live in these parts," Bogie continued, lowering his voice to a whisper. "In fact, many in these parts are still fighting it."

Maximilian looked at Bogie, not quite sure what he meant. "What do you mean?" Maximilian pried. "I thought the Civil War ended slavery in the United States."

Bogie leaned closer and placed the brim of his straw hat over his mouth to hide his words. "Laws that are written thousands of miles away in Washington don't necessarily reach the darker corners of these Louisiana bayous," he said. "The seeds of **prejudice** that led to that war were planted long before Lincoln was elected president. They will take much longer to die than a mere **decade**."

A chill ran up Maximilian's spine, despite the rising temperature on the hurricane deck.

"Enough of this talk," Bogie declared, fanning himself with his hat. "It's Christmas Eve and we have a lot to be thankful for, Mr. Maximilian," he said with renewed enthusiasm. "Let's go inside and see where this music is coming from."

Maximilian nodded in agreement and ran a paw through the fur on his head. He was not used to a warm winter.

"That sounds great, Bogie!" Maximilian said. "I've been wondering about that music ever since I arrived."

"Well, let's make our way back down to the boiler deck. It is where most of the passenger rooms are located. I can show you some of the inside workings of this 'city' on the river," Bogie said with a grin.

The mouse and the frog waited for the right moment to cross the upper deck. Then, they made their way back down the stairs.

Maximilian saw a finely decorated Christmas tree at the front of the hurricane deck. A blue spruce sat to the right of a skylight. It was wound with red and gold ribbon and covered with delicate glass balls and shimmering icicles. Candles with slightly burnt wicks sat on the bows of the tree. Maximilian imagined that when night fell on the river, they would be lit again.

Maximilian loved Christmas. It was his favorite holiday. *If there were ever a time for a Christmas miracle,* he thought, *now would be the perfect time of year.*

Chapter 6:
SEASON'S GREETINGS

The hallway inside the boiler deck was cool and inviting. The same master craftsmanship that Maximilian had seen on the outer decks was within the corridor as well. The crown molding, the beautifully carved chair railing, and the chandeliers were amazing. Each room was labeled with a polished brass plate with the room number.

"This is where the tier one passengers stay," Bogie told Maximilian. "Tier one are the highest paying passengers. These suites are the nicest on the *Belle*."

Maximilian and Bogie hid behind a piece of luggage at the far end of the hallway.

Maximilian guessed that fifteen to twenty rooms were located on this floor. Each door had a sprig of holly fastened to it in the spirit of the Christmas season.

Bogie raised his webbed hand and waved to a small figure halfway down the hallway.

"This is my good pal, Calvin Q. Cricket," Bogie said. He placed a long blade of sweetgrass into his lower lip. It hung from his mouth as he talked.

The long-limbed cricket jumped quickly down the hallway. Within a few seconds, he was introducing himself to Maximilian.

"Season's greetings!" Calvin said, a gray fedora sitting on his head. His legs made up over half of his thin body. A silk vest hung loosely from his frame.

Although Maximilian was enjoying the paddleboat tour Bogie was giving him, he was distracted. He still could not remember what Nathaniel had said about the fuel needed for the time machine.

Maximilian looked at his pocket watch. It was almost noon. He was becoming more and more concerned by the hour.

"Have you had a chance to show our new friend the dining hall yet?" Calvin asked. His hat, fixed with several berries of mistletoe, wobbled on his head as he talked. His voice was heavy with the same accent as Bogie's and he was very **animated**.

"It is a grand sight indeed," Calvin continued. "It will surely be a merry celebration at tonight's party."

Bogie licked his lips. "Well, let's go have a look, Cal," Bogie said.

Maximilian had other ideas. He wanted to investigate the rest of the ship and hopefully jog his memory regarding the fuel source.

"I will meet up with you at tonight's party," Maximilian said. He could not help but be excited for the party. It sounded like a good distraction for him and everything that was on his mind.

"Indeed!" Bogie said. He and Calvin hopped down another corridor toward the center of the boat. Watching them go, the differences in their body shapes and sizes made Maximilian smile.

Rolling up his shirtsleeves, Maximilian thought about which direction he wanted to go. Suddenly, a man emerged from the boiler deck and caught Maximilian's attention.

The man strolled down the hallway toward Maximilian. He passed several **kerosene** lanterns as he went. The light shone off his crisp, white suit.

Maximilian's pulse quickened.

The man in the white suit....

Chapter 7:
THE MAN IN THE WHITE SUIT

Maximilian could not believe his luck. Most of the passengers aboard the *Mississippi Belle* had made their way out onto the **observation decks**. Other passengers were in search of food or entertainment. But here was the man in the white suit.

The man's stride was confident. His outfit seemed to be a perfect reflection of his attitude. Maximilian noticed that he also carried a pocket watch. The silver chain draped from the inside of his vest.

Maximilian watched as the man stopped in front of cabin number 167. Despite having much more serious things on his mind, Maximilian jumped at the opportunity to follow the man. He wanted to find out more about him.

The door was only open for a couple of seconds, but that's all Maximilian needed. He invited himself inside.

Bogie was right. The tier one passengers traveled in luxury. The room was rather large. It was simple with a twin-sized bed, an oak desk, and a dresser. It was quiet in this room. For the first time since he had arrived, Maximilian could not hear the music.

The man removed his coat and hung it on the back of the bathroom door. The bathroom was small with a sink, mirror, and toilet. Although the lights were dimmed, Maximilian was still cautious to remain hidden behind a desk leg.

The man lay on the bed and closed his eyes. Maximilian watched him for several minutes. The only sound in the room was the ticking of the man's watch, which he had hung in a holder on the bed stand next to him. The man's chest rose and fell as his breathing grew heavier. Maximilian decided it was safe to climb the leg of the desk to find out more about his identity.

Thanks to his time machine, Maximilian had spent time with President Lincoln. He had also seen Leland Stanford drive the golden spike of the transcontinental railroad. So, Maximilian was no stranger to people of special significance. He could spot them wherever he went. For some reason, the man in the white suit seemed like a special person, too.

Maximilian climbed the desk as the man began to snore lightly in the background. Once on top, he noticed a writing tablet. Next to it sat a blue ballpoint pen, a silver billfold, and a pair of reading glasses.

Maximilian ran a finger through his whiskers as he examined these items. He considered making his way over to the dresser to find out even more about this stranger. Something on the desk caught his attention before he could.

Maximilian carefully walked over to the man's folded glasses. He stepped onto a pile of papers that were neatly folded on the desk. He was startled slightly as the man rolled onto his side. He froze. The man stayed facing the wall and fell deeper into sleep.

Maximilian went back to investigating the papers on the desk. He saw the cover sheet of what appeared to be a manuscript. He read the title, written neatly in blue ink:

The Adventures of Tom Sawyer
by Mark Twain

Chapter 8:
MR. CLEMENS

"Mark Twain . . . ," Maximilian quietly repeated to himself. He looked at the man sleeping on the bunk several feet away. He scurried around the desk to study the other objects on the small table.

The silver pocket watch had fancy cursive letters on it. Maximilian thought that the letters would be MT for Mark Twain. Instead, the inscription read, "SLC."

Maybe it was a gift, Maximilian thought. He moved on. The man's glasses were folded neatly on the writing pad. When Maximilian looked closer, he found it was covered in notes.

Maximilian studied the comments. Two in particular stood out to him. The first was, *"Nobody deserves to be helped who doesn't try to help himself."* The second read, *"'Faith without works' is a risky **doctrine**."*

Maximilian paused and thought about this for a moment. Mark Twain continued to snore away his afternoon.

Maximilian was now caught in his third **era** by Nathaniel's time machine. He knew he had made a big mistake. The mistake had not been to try and save his home and his family. It had been placing his trust, his life, in the hands of someone he had just met.

In an attempt to save Tanner's Glen from being destroyed, Maximilian had made things more difficult. Worse yet, he might never see his mother and sister again to explain. Yes, this had been the biggest mistake of his life.

Mark Twain's words reminded Maximilian that he'd had few options. While his actions might have seemed extreme at the time, he had been forced to make a decision.

Maximilian struggled to remember what fuel the time machine needed. The answer continued to escape him. Being stuck in 1875 appeared to be more and more of a possibility.

Maximilian cleared his mind. He continued to scan the quotes that Twain had written. Another note caught his attention:

"The Mississippi River towns are comely, clean, well-built, and pleasing to the eye and cheering to the spirit," Twain penned. "The Mississippi Valley is as **reposeful** as a dreamland, nothing worldly about it . . . nothing to hang a fret or a worry upon."

Maximilian sat on his tail. He had only been on the *Mississippi Belle* for a few hours, but he found it friendly and inviting. Bogie and Calvin had been very nice to him.

Suddenly, a knock came from the cabin door. Maximilian jumped up and raced down the desk leg. He hid behind a leather duffle bag sitting on the floor. Twain rustled in his bed, but he failed to wake. After a few seconds, the knocking came again, this time louder.

Twain's eyes slowly opened and he yawned. The knocking had paid off and he was awake.

"Just a moment," Twain called out. He sat up and let out another drowsy yawn. He stretched, his once finely pressed shirt and suit pants were now wrinkled.

For the first time, Maximilian noticed something about Twain. In addition to his white, fuzzy mustache and wild hair, he had large, white eyebrows to match. Maximilian could not help but laugh under his breath.

Mark Twain made his way to the door and opened it. He revealed a shy boy dressed in a black uniform. The boy was holding a tray in his hand.

"Sorry to bother you, sir. I brought your noon tea and cakes, per your request," the boy said.

Twain stood dazed for a second. "Yes, of course," he finally said, still half asleep. "No bother at all, please place it over on the desk." Twain began digging in his pocket.

The boy did as he was told and meekly turned back toward the door. "Before you go," Twain spoke again, "here is a little something extra for your troubles." He handed the boy a gold coin.

The boy's face lit up at once. He thanked Mark Twain nearly a dozen times. "Thank you so much, Mr. Clemens!" he said before disappearing into the hallway.

Twain sat back down on the bed and continued the process of trying to wake up from his nap. Maximilian's thoughts returned to Bogie and to meeting up with him again for the afternoon. Maximilian slid effortlessly under the door.

Maximilian broke into a slight trot once he was back in the corridor. One thing puzzled him greatly. The boy who delivered the tea referred to the man in the white suit as *Mr. Clemens*. The initials on the billfold were *SLC*. So, who exactly was Mark Twain?

Maximilian had managed to answer part of the mystery, but had opened another one in the process. He shook his head and jogged in the direction that Bogie and Calvin had gone just a short time earlier.

Chapter 9:
DECKING THE HALLS

Maximilian scampered down the carpeted hallway. He was careful to dodge the occasional passenger. He ducked in and out of shadows, past a variety of rooms and lobbies. He entered a large room lit brightly by a handsome crystal chandelier.

Maximilian placed his back flat against the wall. He looked around and wondered where Bogie might be in such a grand ballroom.

He looked to the east end and noticed that the room was scattered with games and card tables. Several gray-haired men played cards. At the same time, a pair of gentlemen swapped jokes and pushed stacked chips to the center of a card table.

Smoke **wafted** through the air and Maximilian fought the urge to cough. He did not want to bring attention to himself. He continued to hug the wall as he circled his way around the ballroom.

Over the noise of the **casino**, Maximilian's ears picked up the faint cry of an animated bullfrog. Bogie was trying to get his attention amidst all the noise. Maximilian could see Bogie across the room waving his straw hat and calling his name. Their eyes met and Bogie motioned in his direction.

"Come on, Maximilian!" Bogie yelled. Maximilian scurried toward a small wooden door hidden in the baseboard. Once he was inside, the door was shut behind him and they were inside the walls of the riverboat.

"Follow me," Bogie again instructed. Before Maximilian knew where they were going, they were climbing.

"Critters have been traveling on this river for as long as people have," Bogie said, one hop ahead of Maximilian. "My ancestors helped build these stairs and ramps so that they could get around easier and safer. It's heartbreaking to think that when the *Mississippi Belle* docks for the last time in N'Orleans, she'll be retired. She will never travel these parts again."

It was clear that Bogie was truly saddened by this thought. Maximilian considered all the hard work that must have gone into making the network of stairs they were on.

He could tell they were climbing higher and higher inside the walls. His legs started to cramp. Finally they stopped, having reached the top. When they stepped from inside the plaster walls, Maximilian could see that they had climbed all the way into the rafters of the casino.

The ballroom floor beneath them was impressive. Maximilian's legs weakened from the height at which they stood.

"What a view!" Maximilian said, looking in Bogie's direction.

"It certainly is, my friend," Bogie replied. "In a few short hours, all of these gaming tables will be replaced with dining tables for tonight's Christmas Eve feast."

Everyone seemed to be having a splendid time. Maximilian got the impression that the gamblers were doing more losing than winning.

"**Gambling** has become a big draw to travelers on riverboats," Bogie said. "We're technically not in any one particular state. So, the money that changes hands on this here boat is not subject to the same taxes it otherwise would be," he explained.

Maximilian unbuttoned his vest and patted some dust from his shirt. "Will they remove all of these tables for tonight's dinner?" he asked. "What else do they have planned?" After having seen how fancy everything else was on board the ship, Maximilian could not imagine what they would do for a Christmas party.

"Woo wee!" Bogie cried. His long, pink tongue ran smoothly over his lips. "You cannot imagine the time that will be had in here tonight!" he exclaimed. "Why, there will be music, singing, dancing, and the most delicious dinner you could only dream of, Maximilian! We Southerners know how to throw a proper party." He gave Maximilian a playful slap on the back with his hat.

Maximilian looked around the rafters and began to notice that they were not alone. Bogie's friend Calvin was busy helping a small army of animals and insects set up their own party for the night. A team of ants had carried in long serving tables. At the same time, a heavy-set mole unfolded wooden chairs. Small kerosene lights were being placed at each individual table. In the beams, flying squirrels were busy draping garland and hanging ivy.

Maximilian allowed himself to forget about his troubles and simply enjoy watching the evening's preparations. As the sun reached closer to the western horizon, the afternoon gave way to darkness on the Mississippi River. The riverboat's ballroom transformed into a magical display of Christmas bliss.

Maximilian found a few moments to look out over the calm, murky river by himself. The band in the gallery began to play a lively tune with the familiar rhythm of "Deck the Halls."

"Maximilian, the band just started and boy are they hot tonight!" Bogie called from behind him.

Maximilian turned to go back inside with his new friend. Before he did, he made a Christmas wish to be back home.

Chapter 10:
ONIONS!

The *Mississippi Belle* was alive with energy. Couples dined and danced in the ballroom. They twirled and dipped one another around a beautifully trimmed tree.

Maximilian sat in the rafters watching the joyous celebration of the other riverboat animals. Bogie sat next to him with a glass in one webbed hand and a sprig of holly in the other.

"Certainly a time one wants to be among family and friends," Bogie said, studying Maximilian's expression. The two had yet to discuss family. Though Maximilian had guessed that was one of the reasons Bogie was traveling to New Orleans.

"Christmas is always a special time for my family," Maximilian said. "It's a time to reflect on the previous year and all that we had to be thankful for." Bogie nodded in agreement and took a long drink from his glass.

"Will you be visiting family while you're in New Orleans?" Maximilian asked.

"Most definitely," Bogie said. "I have children in and around the city."

"How many children?" Maximilian asked.

"Well now, let me think," Bogie said. He considered the question long and hard. "I have several dozen small frogs living in a bed of lily pads just on the outskirts of New Orleans. I also have about a hundred or so tadpoles who live just upstream from there in another marsh."

Maximilian's jaw dropped. He thought for a moment how silly his expression must be to Bogie.

"A hundred or so?" Maximilian asked in amazement. Bogie let out a thunderous laugh that caught the attention of every animal at the party. It was **contagious**. Maximilian could not help but laugh along with him. It felt good to laugh. Maximilian's sides hurt as he thought about what Bogie had said.

Calvin eyed both of them. Tipping his fedora he yelled, "Be careful what that frog tells you, Maximilian!" Maximilian and Bogie rolled with laughter, tears streaming down their cheeks.

Suddenly, an electric sound filled the night air. It came from beneath them on the risers where the band was stationed. Maximilian had never heard anything like it before. He sat up, wide-eyed with curiosity.

A drummer and pianist played with a trumpet, a clarinet, and a trombone. Maximilian noticed that the people below were already dancing in a lively fashion.

Bogie tapped his foot in sync with the percussion section of the band. The animals in attendance began dancing as well.

"What band is this?" Maximilian asked. He started to give in to the beat of the song and tap his foot along with Bogie.

Bogie had his eyes closed and listened. "That is the Excelsior Brass Band," he said with his eyes still shut. "The drummer is a

fellow by the name of John Robichaux and the clarinetist is Alphonse Picou." Maximilian watched the two musicians as Bogie named them.

"I've *never* heard music like this!" Maximilian exclaimed. He was amazed at the spell that had been placed over all those in attendance.

All but one person in the entire ballroom were on their feet, clapping in unison.

The man in the white suit, Samuel Clemens, was sitting by himself in the rear of the ballroom. He too seemed to be enjoying this new brand of music . . . in his own way.

"They're on their way to N'Orleans. They are going to try and make it big in the French district," Bogie said. His eyes were open now and he watched the band intently.

"Picou has ridden this line before. I've heard him play on several occasions. Tonight is his best work yet!" Bogie exclaimed. He let out a wild yell from high up in the rafters.

The musicians were dark-skinned and lanky. They moved effortlessly on stage, matching the harmony they played.

Maximilian loved it. His heart was pounding and sweat was starting to stream down his cheeks. It was thrilling! The beat of the snare drum and the sweet notes flying freely from the horns moved him. And, the rhythm of the piano reminded him of his time in Moses's tavern in Gettysburg.

"People and animals in these parts are starting to call this new music *jazz*," Bogie said. He motioned to Calvin, who was moving gracefully to the beat. His long legs and thin torso twisted with every sound.

Cal made his way in their direction. He walked with a strut that kept time with each beat of the drum.

"These guys are amazing!" Maximilian said to Cal. He yelled to be heard.

"They are going to light up New Orleans, I do declare," Cal said. He tipped his hat to them in a gesture of admiration.

"They use all kinds of music to make this sound," Cal said. "Groups like the Excelsior Brass Band are just starting to become **mainstream**, so to speak," he continued. "When they hear this in the music halls of New Orleans, they're going to become real famous."

Bogie went back to dancing. The night seemed to fly by on the *Mississippi Belle*.

Maximilian excused himself and went outside to get some fresh air. Once he was on deck, his pocket watch chimed ten o'clock. A nearly full moon hung high in the night sky. The band continued to play in the background.

The wind felt good on Maximilian's fur and whiskers. He stretched his arms into the air to release the tension from his tired, aching muscles.

Bogie hopped out on the deck behind him. One strap of his overalls was unhooked and his straw hat was missing. Sweat stained his face, but he looked as though he was having the time of his life.

"The night air is refreshing," Maximilian said. "It was getting really warm inside."

Bogie removed his handkerchief from his breast pocket and wiped his face. "Well, some of this sweat isn't from the temperature of the room. It's from Molly Muskrat's famous homemade jambalaya!" he said.

"Really?" Maximilian asked. "I've never had jambalaya before. What's in it?"

Bogie blew his nose on the same handkerchief that he had just used to dry his face. Maximilian cringed.

"Well, it is certainly not a meal for the faint of heart, let me tell you," Bogie began. "But even for a frog with an appetite for flies, it is a treat of a dish. It has all sorts of spices, fish, potatoes, onions . . ."

Maximilian's ears perked up. His heart raced. "What did you just say? What does jambalaya have in it?" he asked.

"Onions," Bogie repeated. "That's probably the other reason I'm crying like a baby!" He laughed at his own joke. Maximilian joined him, but not for the same reason.

"Onions . . . onion juice!" he said softly to himself. "Of course!"

He remembered Nathaniel going over the details of the time machine with him. Maximilian had forgotten that it was the juice from an onion that kept the time machine from "skipping" off line. It also provided the core with its fuel.

Maximilian gave Bogie a grin and a friendly slap on the back. Bogie was somewhat confused but he grinned back at Maximilian.

"I just love onions," Maximilian said with a smile. "Don't you?"

Chapter 11:
DARK STORIES

Maximilian sat beside Bogie for a few more minutes, enjoying the fresh evening air. He still felt relief from having finally determined the solution to his fuel problem.

"A lot of animals say that if you sit real quiet and listen real closely," Bogie began, "you can hear these woods talk."

Maximilian looked at Bogie and asked, "What would the woods say?"

Bogie did not respond right away. The song of the **cicadas** could still be heard from the nearby riverbank.

"They would tell the stories of the slaves. The ones who used the darkness and the cover of these very forests to try and escape the binding chains of their masters," Bogie said. His voice was soft and serious.

The moon dipped behind a cloud at the very moment that Bogie finished his last line. It seemed appropriate, as the tone of the story seemed to take on a rather dark quality.

"If you listen real hard, you can still hear the heavy breathing and the footsteps of slaves running through the underbrush. They were trying to use the Underground Railroad to escape to safety," Bogie said. He turned and looked directly into Maximilian's eyes.

For a moment, Maximilian saw a different side of Bogie. He was unlike the old bullfrog that Maximilian had laughed with earlier.

Maximilian's sensitive ears perked up and rotated in the direction of the forest and the trees. He began listening. He wanted to hear the voices that Bogie spoke of.

"What's the Underground Railroad?" Maximilian asked. "Do you mean like the transcontinental railroad?"

"No, my friend, the Underground Railroad was a network of people who helped escaped slaves flee these parts. They helped them get to places in the North and even to Canada," Bogie said. He eased back on his hind legs to make himself more comfortable.

"The Railroad wasn't run by a single person or a group," he continued. "It consisted of many individuals. Some of them were white, but they were mostly black."

Maximilian watched as the moon returned to the night sky. Its rays shone through the passing trees. Was he seeing things or could he really see people running through the forest as Bogie told his tale?

"Many of the 'conductors' on this system knew only of the local efforts to help runaway slaves. They had very little idea of the overall operation. The railroad had been set up, all up and done the East Coast," Bogie explained. "Many believe that the number of slaves that were successfully removed from these parts of the South was very high."

"How many do they think?" Maximilian asked. He was completely caught up in the story at this point.

"I've heard estimates that range in the tens of thousands," Bogie replied.

"Wow!" Maximilian said in astonishment. "Wasn't it dangerous for those helping the slaves? I mean, would the people running the Underground Railroad get in trouble if someone found out what they were doing?"

"Oh my, yes," Bogie said, shaking his head. "It was very dangerous indeed. So much so

that they risked their own lives if people in these parts found out. **Harboring** or aiding a runaway slave was still against the law back then," he said, raising his voice slightly.

"How do you know so much about this?" Maximilian asked. He made sure that no one around them was **eavesdropping** on their conversation.

Bogie leaned closer to him as he talked. "You'd be awfully surprised by the things I've heard riding this here riverboat all the years, Mr. Maximilian," he said slyly.

"You mentioned the transcontinental railroad," Bogie continued. He was now in full swing sharing his information with his mouse friend. "This network was named the *Underground Railroad* right around 1831. That was when the steam railroads were really beginning to connect the country like never before," he said.

"The terms associated with the actual railroad became code for the different parts of the Underground Railroad," Bogie said. He cut himself short when a noise startled both Maximilian and him.

"Come on," Bogie said suspiciously. "Let's continue this conversation somewhere else."

The clouds again swallowed the light from the stars. As if on cue, darkness fell over the *Mississippi Belle*.

Chapter 12:
MERRY CHRISTMAS

Maximilian moved to the front of the boiler deck. The different riggings were still visible even in the late nighttime hours. The gentle river current could be heard splashing playfully against the lower tiers of the boat.

"You were saying about the words that the actual railroad lent to the underground one, Bogie?" Maximilian said. He prodded the frog to continue his story.

Bogie took one more nervous glance over his shoulder and tried to remember his place. "Yes, of course," he said. "Interestingly enough, the homes and businesses that were safe **havens** for the escaped slaves were referred to as *stations* and *depots*. They were operated by *stationmasters*."

Maximilian found all of this fascinating. He loved hearing about the Underground Railroad.

"Those who contributed money or goods to the effort were *stockholders*," Bogie said. "Finally, it was the *conductor* that had the dangerous job of moving **fugitives** from one station to the next," he said.

"The stockholders were the ones who funded a lot of this operation? Were they like the owners of a company?" Maximilian asked, placing his hands in his pockets.

"Absolutely right," Bogie said in his Southern accent. "Fugitive slaves would also be moved by train and boat—some very similar to the *Belle*," he said. "And that wasn't cheap. Money was also needed to change the appearances of the runaways so they wouldn't be recognized."

This suggestion made perfect sense. It was something that had bothered Maximilian since Bogie started telling him about the Underground Railroad.

"A black man, woman, or child in tattered, ragged clothing would attract attention," Bogie explained. "The donated money purchased new clothes for them—a new beginning altogether."

Maximilian's pocket watch chimed midnight. Its sweet melody was a welcome interruption from the serious conversation that he and Bogie had been sharing.

"Midnight," Maximilian proclaimed. "You know what that means," he said.

"Merry Christmas, my friend!" Bogie yelled. He was no longer concerned with who might overhear them.

"Merry Christmas to you too, Bogart!" Maximilian said. The two shared a hug.

It dawned on Maximilian that Bogie was the first bullfrog he had ever known. The two had bonded almost immediately. Maximilian was truly enjoying their time together.

It was Christmas Day and Maximilian's thoughts returned to home. He would allow himself a few more minutes of holiday cheer in the ballroom with his friends before retiring for the night. He would be making a very important trip to the boat's kitchen in the morning.

The Excelsior Brass Band struck a new chord. Maximilian made his way back into the party behind Bogie.

While he was gazing at the river, Maximilian had formed a plan—a plan that would hopefully take him back to Tanner's Glen.

Chapter 13:
A NEW DAY

After the party, Maximilian walked the lonely hall of the hurricane deck with a little extra spring in his step. The memory he had uncovered that evening had removed a huge weight from his shoulders.

The ship's kitchen would surely have onions. He would only need to borrow a very small amount in order to refuel the time machine. With any luck, he would be able to depart in the morning. But first, he might just have a few minutes to stop by the room of Samuel Clemens. He could use one final **inspirational** quote from his writing tablet.

It was late as Maximilian made his way down another deck. His overcoat still smelled of sweet candied yams, jellied desserts, and other holiday delights from the evening's festivities.

Maximilian took stock of all of his adventures since departing Nathaniel's workshop that fateful night. He had befriended so many fascinating animals and witnessed so many inspiring events. He would never be the same mouse.

Maximilian returned to the time machine around one in the morning. He was relieved to find it exactly as he had left it.

"The juice of an onion," he said out loud. He ran a paw over the finely polished exterior shell.

Maximilian decided to sleep outside in the warm winter weather. He carefully removed his jacket and folded it for a pillow. Two kerosene lanterns hung from exposed hooks on the rear of the boat. They shed just enough light for Maximilian to carry out his regular routine of writing in his journal before turning in. It had become his favorite time of day. He was eager to write down the day's events.

With the heading, *Merry Christmas*, Maximilian wrote quickly. His small paw tried hard to keep up with his thoughts. He wrote about the wisdom of Samuel Clemens. He described the fun-loving grin of a Southern bullfrog named Bogart and his tour of a grand Mississippi River paddleboat. He even included the Christmas celebration that would not soon be forgotten.

The lead on Maximilian's pencil ran low and smooth as he finished his last line. He closed the leather book on another entry. Then, he laid his head on the woolen sleeve of his coat and closed his eyes.

Maximilian's legs twitched, his whiskers flinched, and his muscles tensed as he slowly entered a state of dreaming . . .

Maximilian walked along the familiar path through the brush of Tanner's Glen. Brown hemlock needles cushioned each step. The sun shone bright and warm on his face and he turned his gaze to the gleaming rays of sunshine.

A dark and threatening cloud suddenly overwhelmed the sun and its rays of hope.

The glen became black and cold. An eastern wind blew the weeping cattails on their sides.

Shadows surrounded Maximilian as he turned his collar up. He quickened his pace along the path. His heart pounded harder and harder.

The shadows merged and blocked the end of the trail. Maximilian stopped and looked behind him. More shadows were overtaking his path. Thunder rolled and flashes of lightning crashed through the tall oaks and ashes.

Maximilian watched in amazement as an object slowly entered the light. He could not believe his eyes. The piece of equipment was familiar to him. And now it threatened the very thing he held dearest to his heart. Rolling mightily on its heavy, metal treads and destroying everything in its path was . . . a bulldozer.

The machine moved slowly toward him, tearing the ground as it went. Maximilian searched for a way to escape, but he soon realized there was no escape.

Maximilian woke from his sleep suddenly. He was drenched in sweat. It was morning now, but Maximilian felt exhausted. The nightmare, similar to that of the previous night, was haunting him.

Tired or not, Maximilian had no time to waste. He tossed his coat into the time machine and stretched his arms toward the brilliant blue sky.

This is the day, he thought.

He adjusted his tail behind him and headed in the direction of the boiler deck where the kitchen was located.

Chapter 14:
EXPLORE.
DREAM.
DISCOVER.

Maximilian ran toward the kitchen. The *Mississippi Belle* would be arriving in New Orleans in a few hours. He wanted to avoid any unexpected issues that might arise as passengers and luggage were unloaded at port. Maximilian traced the same course he had with Bogie. This time, however, he took a quick **detour** to a familiar passenger's quarters.

Cabin number 167 was not too far from where Maximilian expected the kitchen to be. The dark oak door to the cabin was closed. When Maximilian pressed his ear to it, he heard nothing.

No shuffling of feet, no rustling of papers, and no voices. There was silence inside.

The bottom of the closed door was just far enough off the ground. Maximilian laid flat on his stomach, arched his back, and carefully pulled himself inside.

To his amazement, the room was completely empty. They had not yet docked at their destination, so Maximilian was baffled. There

were no signs that the room had been used at any point during the cruise.

The closet was empty except for a few clothes hangers. The bed was neatly made, the sheets creased and the pillows fluffed. The desk that Maximilian had examined less than twenty-four hours earlier was bare of Samuel Clemens's belongings. The chair was pushed in. A wave of disappointment swept over Maximilian.

What had it been about Samuel Clemens that had **mesmerized** Maximilian?

His handwritten words of wisdom had certainly stuck with Maximilian. Since keeping his own diary, Maximilian had also come to hold writers with special regard. Mr. Clemens was a man that impressed Maximilian as being a source of insight. Maximilian was sure he was a splendid storyteller.

Just as Maximilian was preparing to leave, something caught his attention. A crumpled piece of paper was in the wastebasket at the foot of the bed. Based on how neat the rest of the room was, it must have been thrown away just before the room had been cleared.

Maximilian's interest pulled him the full width of the room. Certainly he could not leave without seeing what it was first. After all, it was probably nothing but a mere scrap piece of paper.

Maximilian climbed to the lip of the wastebasket. Careful not to tip the garbage over on himself, Maximilian took the wrinkled paper in his paw. He jumped to the floor and laid the paper out in front of him. He ironed out creases and smoothed it as best he could.

It was, in fact, Samuel Clemens's handwriting. The paper was covered with notes and doodles. One, in particular, had been framed in a box. Maximilian read it aloud:

Twenty years from now you will be more disappointed by the things that you didn't do than by the ones you did do. So . . . Explore. Dream. Discover.

Maximilian stopped and thought about the words of Clemens. He licked his finger and began to carefully tear out the quote. He was happy to see it also included a signature.

The beautiful, moving words could not be left behind or worse yet, in the trash. No, that simply was not acceptable to Maximilian. He would have to find room for this newfound treasure in the limited space of the time machine. He would have to decide what he wanted to keep and what he could bare to part with.

Samuel Clemens's autograph and quote would make a nice addition to the growing collection from his trip. It was a rather impressive collection, which already included a button of President Abraham Lincoln and a nugget of gold from Silver Springs, Utah.

Gently folding the piece of paper and placing it under his arm, Maximilian could not help but smile. He slid back under the door into the hallway and continued toward the kitchen.

Maximilian was more determined than ever to find what he needed and continue on with his adventure. The fate of his home depended on it.

Chapter 15:
MOUSE!

The smell of freshly sliced, wood-smoked bacon frying practically lifted Maximilian off of his paws. The smell floated down the hallway from the kitchen. Maximilian was still full to the brim from last night's feast. But, his mouth watered and his stomach growled at the smell that filled the boat's corridor.

Maximilian tried not to think about what he would do if there were no onions left in the kitchen. There was also the problem of not knowing what amount of onion juice was necessary to refuel the time machine's battery. He decided that he would deal with these issues later.

By the time Maximilian reached the kitchen, breakfast preparation was in full swing. Several cooks and waiters were dashing around one another, trying to meet the demands of their tables.

Maximilian would have to be very cautious. Now was certainly not the time to make a mistake. It would be a mistake that could very well cost him his life. If there was one place in particular that mice and other "vermin" were not welcome, it was a kitchen. He would have to keep his wits about him.

The bustling excitement inside the kitchen and the clinking of pots and pans were distracting. Maximilian also found it difficult to navigate along the slippery tile floor. He paused to consider his next move.

Maximilian tried hard to use every cutting board, waiter tray, and serving cart as a hiding place. At the same time, he made sure to keep the poetic words from cabin 167 carefully protected under his arm.

A line of three or four chefs caught the attention of Maximilian. They were working at the far end of the kitchen with their backs to everyone else. Maximilian could hear the rhythmic sound of chopping and cutting. He noticed that they were helping to make omelets for the morning menu. Surely onions would have to be included in their recipe.

Scurrying up the leg of a metal counter, Maximilian carefully placed the folded piece of paper inside the front of his shirt and wiped the sweat from his paws. It was hot in the kitchen and Maximilian's nerves were beginning to get the best of him.

He took a deep breath and scanned the countertop. Immediately he saw a stack of carrots waiting to be washed in the sink, a mound of mushrooms with their tops removed, and several finely ripened tomatoes. They all looked very appealing, but there were no onions.

Maximilian's heart began to pound. The thought crept into his mind that maybe there just weren't any onions left from last night's stew.

Everyone in the kitchen was on task and busy. The chefs stationed at the cutting boards worked like a well-trained army. Maximilian decided to make his way down the shiny, stainless steel counter toward a large lobster pot.

Maximilian lifted his nose toward the ceiling and took two lengthy whiffs. He could smell warm, browning flapjacks on the stove. There was also the smell of the bacon grease sitting on the range. He could just make out the strong, **distinctive** odor of onions!

Maximilian felt an immediate sense of relief. Several large, white onions came into view on the far side of the kitchen. He placed his paw over his chest in an attempt to slow his racing heartbeat.

Maximilian's heart had not had long to rest when it jumped back into his throat. He began to step carefully out from behind the cooking pot. Just then, he heard the words he had most dreaded.

"MOUSE!" a startled cook yelled. The cook turned immediately and grabbed a spatula from the drying rack next to him. He raised it over his head and rushed toward Maximilian. The other startled chefs threw their accusing glares in his direction as well.

Maximilian froze in fear.

Chapter 16:
A CLOSE CALL

The metal spatula came down hard on the counter behind Maximilian. It just missed the tip of his tail. The gust of air nearly blew him over. Maximilian saw the cook raise his hand again and prepare to take a second swipe.

The activity of the early morning breakfast rush had nearly come to a halt. Everyone had turned their attention to Maximilian. For a split second Maximilian thought he saw Bogie behind a coffee tin ready to come to his aid. But there was no help this time. He had only himself to rely on.

A burly chef with one of the taller hats in the kitchen threw a soup ladle in disgust. "Filthy pests, I thought we had this taken care of before we left Vicksburg!" he yelled. His voice was draped in a heavy French accent. "This is why this riverboat is being retired!"

Maximilian's legs were tiring. He wanted to find a hiding place to rest and catch his breath. An overturned pasta strainer gave him that chance. With a quick flip of his paw, he found himself cowering underneath the strainer. He peered out through one of the circular draining holes.

The chefs chasing him stood with their hands on their hips. They were **dumbfounded** at his disappearance. His shirt clung to his fur with sweat. He could feel the paper with Samuel Clemens's writing on it soaked and stuck to his side.

Maximilian's burning lungs continued to work overtime. He moved to the other side of the strainer to find the onions. The chase that had threatened his life had managed to get him even closer to his goal. He remained focused on getting several peels of one of those beautiful vegetables.

As quickly as everyone had dropped what they were doing to chase their uninvited breakfast guest, the staff returned to cooking. Between the colander and the onions, Maximilian could see a large bag of flour, a basket of eggs, and a burlap sack of coffee beans. Each of these things would be perfect to screen his movement to the white onions.

Maximilian did not want to wait. He estimated that it must be going on ten o'clock in the morning.

Taking one last deep breath, he lifted the drainer's handle. He made his way quickly, but watchfully, to the bag of flour several feet away. Reaching the bag safely was only step one.

From here, Maximilian moved to the wicker basket of soft brown eggs. Hiding in the shadow of the basket, Maximilian noticed that a trail of flour paw prints were now tracing every step he took. He took a second to wipe his feet. He hoped no one would notice the white paw marks that spotted the counter.

Next, Maximilian raced to the bag of French-roasted coffee beans. He loved the smell of coffee and these were some of the nicest beans he had ever smelled. More importantly, they sat next to the onions.

Up to this point, Maximilian had managed to remain undetected. He was more worried now though, as he had to grab several layers of the onion before making his escape. The time machine sat patiently waiting for him.

Maximilian straightened and whispered reassuringly to himself, "You can do this. You can do this . . ."

There would be at least a few seconds between the coffee beans and the onions when he was completely exposed. But he had no other choice. Maximilian ran as fast as his weary legs could carry him into the open and toward his ticket home.

Chapter 17:
MISSION ACCOMPLISHED

Maximilian could not remember what ran through his head before he dashed out from behind the coffee. It all happened very quickly. With his back flat against the onions, he could smell their strong, bold scent.

Maximilian's heart continued to pound. He did not hear any new sounds from the prep area. He slid a single fingernail through the skin of the onion and slowly began to slide it downward. He felt as though he was cutting three or four layers of onion.

Maximilian had gone through so much to get to this point. He wanted to make sure he took enough to fully refuel the battery. It certainly would not hurt if he took more than he needed.

As he slowly pulled the seams of the onion apart, Maximilian could feel some moisture building on his hand. His eyes began to water. He used his shirtsleeve to wipe away the tears.

Through blurry, irritated eyes, Maximilian took one last look around the kitchen. The cooks, chefs, and waiters remained distracted. He thought that maybe they had forgotten about him.

The head French chef still seemed rather angry as he supervised the lower-ranking cooks. His one eyebrow stood at attention as he looked suspiciously over the shoulder of a slender cook with an especially young face.

"Where are the onions?" the head chef asked. He threw up his hands in disgust. "How can you possibly make this without onions?" he continued to rant.

That was all Maximilian needed to hear. He darted to the floor and out the closest door back into the hallway.

Maximilian had managed to get three decent-sized pieces of onion. He was sure that would be enough to replenish the time machine's energy.

Maximilian made his way down the carpeted hallway one final time. He took in the fine molding, woodwork, and wallpaper. His time on the riverboat had definitely been like nothing he had ever experienced before.

Maximilian ran down the stairs leading from the hurricane deck to the loading deck. Soon, he was on the rear of the boat where the impressive paddle wheel was located.

The Christmas spirit lingered in the air. Garland still hung on the railing of the loading deck. Holly berry sprigs still clung to cabin doors.

Finally, Maximilian reached the back of the boat. The time machine looked the same as the first time he had laid eyes on it in Nathaniel's workshop. He removed the folded paper from his vest and carefully placed it behind the driver's seat. He took out a **canteen** he had brought from home and decided it could be left behind. This would provide the room he needed for his new find.

Maximilian began to examine the outside of the time machine. Its glossy acorn shell was warm from the morning heat. The casing was smooth and seamless with one tiny exception. On the right side of the time machine capsule, Maximilian found a small opening covered by a cap made out of peach pit. He thought this had to be where the time machine's fuel went.

Turning and removing the cap, Maximilian grabbed the first piece of onion. He rolled it like a newspaper. Then, Maximilian began to twist the onion slice. He tried hard to wring out any amount of fluid he could.

Maximilian's tiny arms strained. He managed to get just four drops of juice into the fuel spout. It was not an easy process. Maximilian wondered just how much of the juice actually went into the machine as he watched a lone drop roll onto the ground.

There was only one way to find out. Maximilian climbed through the portal hatch and turned the ignition. He held his breath as the control panel came to life. The darkness inside the pod glowed red from the dashboard lights.

First, the 'Year' light came on, and then the 'Month' indicator. Finally, the 'Day' display lit up. Maximilian tried to contain the excitement that was beginning to build inside him.

Just as he was ready to climb back out to gather his things for departure, another light switched on in front of him. Maximilian closed his eyes as his stomach sank.

Low fuel.

Chapter 18:
ONE MORE TRY

Maximilian carefully left the portal and grabbed another piece of the onion. He headed back to the fuel tank. Following the same process as before, he used all of his might. He squeezed a few more drops of juice into the time machine.

Maximilian replaced the peach pit tank cap for a second time. He climbed back through the hatch and began the start-up procedure again. The lights lit on cue. Maximilian prepared for the worst. But nothing happened! The fuel warning light remained off. Maximilian felt an enormous sense of relief.

It was time.

It seemed everything was always about time with Maximilian. Knowing that he was ready to try his luck at making it back home to Tanner's Glen made him almost giddy.

Maximilian made one final examination of the time machine. As he did, he looked out over the railing of the *Mississippi Belle* one last time. The wooden paddle wheel continued to turn in the mighty Mississippi River.

Maximilian heard a soft voice over his shoulder.

"The boat will be docking within the hour," Bogie said. "You have the look in your eye of someone who's already moving on."

Maximilian smiled. He looked out at the low-hanging willow trees on the riverbank.

"You certainly have proven to be quite the Southern gentle-frog," Maximilian said.

"I hope the upcoming New Year is kind to you, young sir," Bogie said. He gave Maximilian a polite tip of his hat.

The two exchanged well wishes and parted ways. Maximilian watched as the round frog hopped back down the deck of the paddleboat and slowly out of sight.

Two long blasts from the captain's whistle slowed the churning paddle wheel. The port of New Orleans was a stone's throw away.

Maximilian wanted to leave before the **chaos** of passengers unloading began.

Drawing in one final breath of fresh air, Maximilian climbed back into the time machine. He sat on his neatly folded coat and fastened his seat belt. He locked the portal door and began the start-up sequence.

2013, October, 15, Tanner's Glen.

Maximilian braced himself. His paws clenched the chair arms tightly, threatening to leave nail marks in the arms. He kept his gaze squarely on the desired date and destination.

The time machine began to spin and seemed to be working as it had every other time. His head ached and his body strained, but all the time, Maximilian refused to close his eyes.

Chapter 19:
ANOTHER BOAT

The time machine came to a smooth stop. Maximilian was relieved when the low fuel emergency light remained off. Hopefully he would not have to go through that stressful ordeal again. But if he did, at least he knew what fuel to use.

Maximilian removed his seat belt. Suddenly, he was thrown into the side of the time machine. He took a minute to catch his bearings. His shoulder had hit the wall hardest and began to throb.

What on earth had just happened? Where was he?

Maximilian sat in the cockpit for another minute to see if the jarring would happen again. When it seemed safe, he opened the hatch with his handkerchief and climbed out.

It was almost pitch black. And it felt as though he were on a cloud, floating over the ground.

Maximilian tried to steady himself and regain his balance. Before he knew it, he was flat on his back, looking at the time machine. It teetered back and forth after another violent jolt.

Maximilian was starting to worry. Wherever he had found himself this time, both himself and Nathaniel's invention were in danger. If the time machine was damaged, he was lost forever in time.

Getting to his paws, Maximilian tried to spot clues as to where he was. He found he had landed among towering stacks of trunks and boxes. The air quality was very poor. Maximilian used his handkerchief to cover his sensitive nose and protect it from the dust that was in the air.

The movement under his paws was familiar. Maximilian stopped and thought for a moment. Was it the harsh rocking of an old, rickety wagon like that of the Franklins' on their trip out West? It seemed different than that, and even more familiar. It felt, almost, like he was on a boat!

Chapter 20:
A FRUSTRATED MOUSE

Maximilian could not believe it. The feeling he had now was most definitely that of being on water. But it wasn't the calm, slow-moving tides of the Mississippi River. The inside of this ship was nothing like the beautifully crafted ship he had just left.

The time machine had failed again. Maximilian was just as disappointed and frustrated as the previous times. But, he did not have time to **wallow**.

What he thought must be another rather large wave rocked the boat. Maximilian's stomach dropped to his feet, a feeling he was not at all fond of.

Eyeing a nearby crate, Maximilian scurried up it. He used the wooden hatches like the rungs of a ladder. He climbed and climbed until he reached the top. What he saw next was absolutely heart-wrenching.

The ship he was in was carrying hundreds, maybe thousands, of people. They were all tightly pressed next to one another. Maximilian saw men, women, and children of all ages sitting on top of one another.

These were not the wealthy passengers of a fine, Southern paddleboat. These people looked scared and desperate. This huddled mass looked tired and **downtrodden**.

Maximilian climbed back down from the crate. He nearly slipped on more than one occasion, rattled from what he had just seen.

He made his way through the boxes and bags and back to the time machine. He would wait the day out inside it if he needed to. At least there he felt safe.

As he turned the corner of the last crate, he neared the time machine. Maximilian saw something else that sent a shock of fear through his body. With one more lurch of the boat, Maximilian watched in horror as the time machine swayed to one side.

It teetered unsteadily for a brief moment and then tipped over with a loud crash.

About
the Mississippi River

The sprawling railroad tracks that were slowly covering the country had not been the first method of travel in the United States. The other "highway" that helped define American culture in the nineteenth century was the mighty Mississippi River.

The Mississippi River divided the United States. Those who traveled its waters and lived along its banks developed a unique culture all their own.

Countless boats traveled up and down the Mississippi's muddy waters each year. They were an important piece in the US economy and culture.

The most famous tales of life on the Mississippi were told by American writer Mark Twain. His popular characters Tom Sawyer and Huckleberry Finn entertained countless readers. Their adventures along the famed river came to represent the carefree spirit of life in the 1890s.

The country was healing through years of Reconstruction. It was expanding the nation's boundaries west as well. The renewed sense of lightheartedness was reflected in Twain's stories and cultural movements like the Jazz Age.

America had developed into a truly cultural "melting pot." Its people continued to look for new and creative ways to express their freedom.

Glossary

acquaintance - someone you have met briefly.

animated - full of movement or activity.

architect - a person who plans and designs something.

buoy - a ring-shaped flotation device used to save people in the water.

canteen - a container for liquid, usually water.

casino - a place where adults go to bet money on games.

chaos - a state of total confusion.

cherish - to hold dear.

cicada - a large, flylike insect with transparent wings.

compliment - a feeling or expression of praise or liking for something.

compressor - a machine that presses together gases.

contagious - spreading easily from one person to another.

debris - bits and pieces of rocks.

decade - a measurement of time equal to ten years.

detour - to take a different route.

distinctive - something that sets one apart from others.

doctrine - a principle or position in a way of thinking or acting.

dominate - to control by the use of power; to rise above.

downtrodden - suffering from being held back.

drastic - with extreme action.

dumbfounded - to be confused and astonished.

eavesdrop - to listen secretly to a private conversation.

era - a period of time or history.

fugitive - a person trying to escape.

gambling - betting money on games such as cards or slot machines.

harbor - to give shelter or refuge to someone.

haven - a place of safety and shelter.

hospitality - having a welcoming and pleasant environment.

hurricane roof - a deck at the top of a passenger ship.

hydraulics - the force of liquid, which is used to make machines move.

inspirational - inspiring; uplifting.

kerosene - a flammable oil.

layman - a person who does not belong to a certain profession or is not an expert in a field.

mainstream - to be known or familiar to everyone.

mesmerized - to be hypnotized or unable to look away from something.

observation deck - an area near the top of a building or ship from which people can see the surrounding area.

parasol - a lightweight umbrella used to shade one from the sun.

prejudice - hatred of a particular group based on factors such as race or religion.

reposeful - at ease or relaxed.

statehouse - a room on a ship where a passenger stays.

transcontinental - crossing a continent.

unsavory - unpleasant or disagreeable.

waft - to move or go lightly on the wind.

wallow - to become or remain helpless.

About the Author

Maximilian P. Mouse, Time Traveler was created by Philip M. Horender. Horender resides in upstate New York with his wife, Erin, and their dog, MoJo.

Horender earned his Bachelor of Arts in History with a minor in education from St. Lawrence University. He later obtained his Masters in Science in Education from the University at Albany, the State University of New York.

He currently teaches high school history, coaches swimming, and advises his school's history club. When he is not writing, Horender enjoys biking, kayaking, and hiking with Erin and MoJo.